T0199183

Fred Lipsius

The Tree With Many Colors

To order additional copies of this book, contact:
Xlibris
1-888-795-4274
www.Xlibris.com
Orders@Xlibris.com

ISBN: Softcover   978-1-7960-9235-6
        Hardcover   978-1-7960-9236-3
        EBook   978-1-7960-9234-9

Library of Congress Control Number: 2020904457

Print information available on the last page

Rev. date: 05/05/2020

Thanks to Kathleen Claycomb, Mike Carrera, the Richard family (Stacey, Ted, and Sophia), and my wife, Setsuko, for their feedback and helpful suggestions to improve my book.

A very special thanks is extended to Sri Harold Klemp.

This tree has more beautiful colors than any tree anywhere! It's a very old tree. No one seems to know just how old it really is. The tree has all these beautiful colors to simply attract children and adults to it. And there's a reason why. It's here to help open the heart of each person who stops by the tree or sits or rests under it.

The tree gives a special gift of love to each one who enjoys its beauty. Unusual, wondrous things happen for them. For example, if you have a question and you think of it, whisper it, or ask the question out loud, the tree may give you the answer but in a very unexpected way. A gentle breeze may pass by and touch you like a soft kiss. Then you will understand what the tree is saying without any words being said. Or if something is really bothering you a lot, the tree may let you know how to make things better. No one seems to know just how or why the tree can do this. It's been quite a mystery for a very long time.

One summer morning, a nine-year-old boy named Hugh woke up from sleep, very excited. He had the feeling that he was going to have a big adventure. The day before, he had heard some people talking about a special tree in the park near his house. Hugh had been to this park many times with his family but had never seen this special tree. All morning, he kept thinking about the tree and wanted to see it. So he asked his parents if he could go to the park all by himself to look for the tree. They said yes. So he left his house, waved to his mom and dad, and very happily walked to the park.

When he got there, he looked around to find the tree. There were lots of trees but no unusual one, so he kept looking. After a while, Hugh started to get tired and very thirsty. Nearby, he found a water fountain. As he raised his head from the fountain after drinking, he noticed something on a small hill not far away. The sun was shining brightly over something very large. Hugh couldn't see what it was because of the very strong sunlight, so he went over to get a closer look. When he got there, he suddenly stopped with an amazed look on his face. And for a moment, he felt like he was in another world.

He was standing in front of a very big tree filled with all kinds of very bright colored leaves and wonderful-smelling flowers. All types of birds were flying around the tree. Some landed on the branches. Hugh began to count the purple leaves high up on the tree but soon stopped because there were just too many leaves for him to count. Then he walked around to the other side of the tree and saw lots of strange kinds of fruits he had never seen before. Just then, a group of birds started singing. Their combined songs were so pretty sounding and so relaxing to Hugh that he felt sleepy. He was also tired from so much walking. So he sat under the tree with his back against the trunk, slowly closed his eyes, and soon fell asleep. Then he had a dream.

He was flying through a huge, colorful galaxy filled with sparkling, twinkling stars of all sizes. It was so much fun! Hugh felt so happy and free.

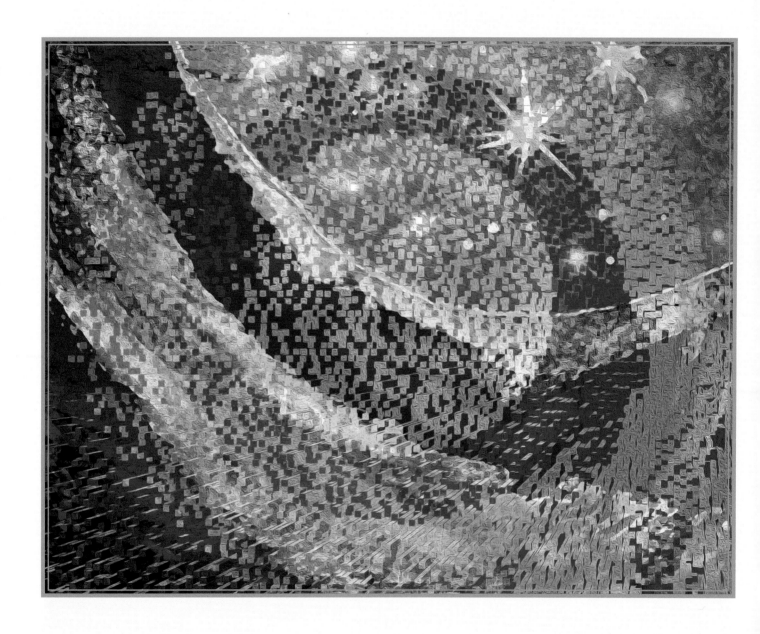

He passed two strange-looking objects that seemed to be playing a game with each other.

Then off in the distance, Hugh noticed a tiny blue dot. It started coming toward him. As it got closer, he saw that it was a person with a blue face with other colors and wearing a red hat with a feather sticking up.

Hugh had never seen anyone with a blue face or ever thought that one could exist! But he didn't feel afraid because this person looked friendly, very wise, and even strangely familiar to him.

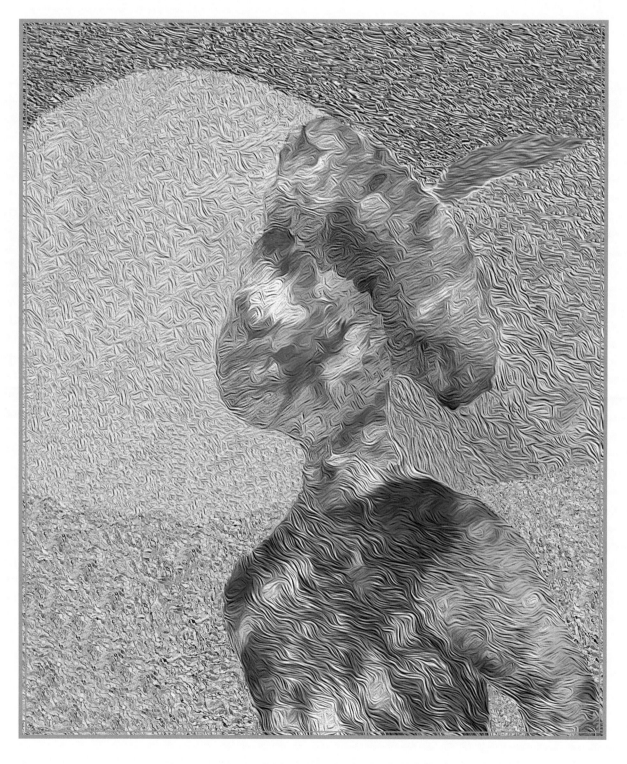

When the blue-faced person got close to Hugh, he smiled for a moment and then held out his hand. Hugh took his hand, and together, they slowly glided down and landed on a small star.

The person spoke, "My name is Teebar. You can call me Tee if you like. I am someone from the very distant past who you once knew. It's been a long, long time since we've seen each other. But I am most happy to see you and be with you again. It's the right time now for us to meet again. You don't remember this, but you've lived many times before in many different bodies and in many different places throughout the universe. I have come to you now because you're ready to learn the many lessons of love. If you allow me, I will teach them to you. Do I have your permission?"

Hugh looked deeply into Teebar's eyes for what seemed like an eternity and felt a strange closeness with him. Then Hugh smiled and said, "Yes, you have my permission."

"Very good," said Teebar. "Now since you are still young and there are so many lessons to learn about love, I will only talk to you about some of them, so you don't get confused or lose interest in what I'm saying. But I want you to know that someday, after you've learned and mastered these lessons, as I have done, you will find happiness beyond anything you ever thought was possible! This I promise you. OK, let's begin."

"Each person eventually finds love, but it usually takes a very long time for most. There's really no rush though, because someday, each person will become a lover of life."

"What's a lover of life?" asked Hugh.

Teebar said, "It's a person who helps others in lots of different ways because they feel love inside themselves. So they naturally want to share or give love to others. They have no other reason to do this. It's not selfish at all. It's just a very pure thing to do. This is part of the reason why we are here—why we exist. It's to give ourselves to life. The other reason why we're here—and this is just as important—is to be able to receive love. So the whole purpose of life is simply to give and receive love. And there are many ways to do this.

"Love has been, is, and will always be here forever. Love can never die, but many people are not able to see it, hear it, or feel it. And many others don't even care to know about it. They cannot accept love or give love. You were often like this long ago, not caring and having certain attitudes and habits that only hurt you and others. You simply made poor choices. But I, Teebar, your old friend from long ago, am here to guide and teach you how and where to find love so you can get rid of these bad habits and attitudes you've been carrying with you for so long."

Teebar continued, "Love is everywhere. It's life itself. Love is in every moment that we live. It's very important that you learn to be aware of love in your life."

"How can I do that, Tee?" asked Hugh.

"Love can be found in the ways we speak, think, and act. Here are some simple examples: petting an animal, watering some flowers, or smiling at someone. Things like that can give you a warm feeling inside. They bring you love and joy as you bring love to others. Can you tell me a way that you enjoy giving?"

"Well, sometimes I open a door for a very old person," Hugh replied.

"Very good," said Teebar. "Have you ever noticed that you really feel good when you do that?"

"Yeah, I guess so," Hugh said, "but I never thought about it before."

"Give love in as many ways as you can, and you will find love coming back to you!"

Teebar continued, "Having good, positive thoughts will keep away the bad, harmful, fearful thoughts. So try to make good choices with your words, thoughts, and deeds. Be a *shining* example to others, just like the bright, twinkling stars we see in the galaxy around us."

"It's also important that you follow your inner feelings and nudges."

"What's a nudge?" asked Hugh.

Teebar said, "A nudge can be a feeling or an idea that you suddenly get or even a soft voice within you letting you know what to do or how to act about something."

"It's like getting a secret *clue* for making good decisions. Yesterday, when you heard people talking about a special tree in the park, you had a *feeling* or desire this morning to find the tree. Life was giving you a nudge inside yourself to go and find it. And because you followed the nudge, you actually found the tree, had this dream, and met me! So you had an *adventure*, just like you felt you would this morning. That's how nudges work. You received a loving gift from life. But remember, only follow your good nudges, not the bad ones."

"Another lesson about love is to be patient and kind to yourself. Try not to let yourself get so upset when something bothers you, like when you don't get *your way* with something. Often, other people have better and easier ways to do things than you. And if you're having trouble understanding something, don't think you *failed* because life is about learning and growing. Making mistakes is how we all learn to do things better, and our mistakes often help us become stronger and more confident that we *can* do things that we didn't think we could do. So practice treating yourself and others better, and this includes animals, rocks, plants, and other things that exist."

"A simple way to receive love is to appreciate the things you have. Sometime, make a list of the things you have that you really like or love. Then be *thankful* for them. Just for a moment, try thinking of something that you love … Now imagine *not* having it. Wouldn't you miss it a lot? So remember to be thankful. Imagine yourself opening a door very wide to let lots of good, happy thoughts and ideas come to you … Always try to keep this door open. Say to yourself, "The door is wide open"… "The door is wide open."

"OK, let's now take a journey into the past to learn some things that will be very helpful for you to know. Hold my hand and let me take you there."

"The Tree with Many Colors that you sat under came from *The Worlds of Color*, where you and I first met. These worlds contained only the purest colors of love known in all the universes."

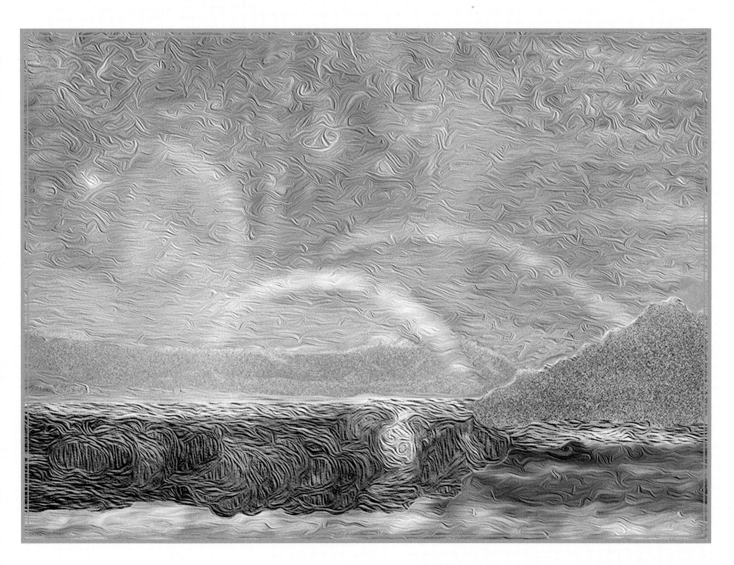

"Our ancestors, those who wore hats with a feather on the top like mine, planted The Tree with Many Colors on the earth to *remind* children and adults of all ages who visit the tree how to love more fully. Most people have forgotten who they are. The tree helps remind them and gives love to people whose hearts are pure. Those who visit this tree with a childlike attitude learn more about who they truly are and what their life's purpose is, as I shared with you earlier."

"Do you mean to give and receive love?" Hugh asked.

"Yes, exactly," said Teebar. "I'm very happy you remember that!"

"The Tree with Many Colors changes its colors, beautiful flowers, and fruits each year."

"Why does it do that, Tee?" Hugh asked.

"It's to *remind* people to stay *open* and not get upset when things change in their life, because life is naturally *changing* all the time. Day turns into night, and night into day. It rains, but then the sun comes out. We cry, we laugh, we get sad, but then we're happy again! So we're always changing, just like life does. But we need to flow freely and joyfully with the many different changes that life brings.

"You will have learned much if you can *accept* the many changes of life—the ups and downs. So don't expect things to always stay the same or be just the way *you* like. Life simply isn't like this, and we can't control it. But if you can accept the things that love brings, whether they seem good or bad to you, then you'll find that many things simply won't bother you anymore."

Hearing Teebar say this made Hugh feel very happy. He had a big smile on his face.

"There is a loving power that cares for all of us much more than we can imagine, and it's often a mystery how it works. But please remember this: the changes in life always happen for our own good, never to hurt us in any way. They are wonderful blessings. So don't be afraid or resist. Just be thankful for whatever life may bring, for it's always teaching us—helping each of us to grow into better, wiser, and more loving people. Life is a great teacher, and our learning never ends—it just goes on and on and on.

"Whenever you are feeling bad or afraid or are having a difficult time, you can simply think of me. Just fill yourself with love, sing my name—Teebar or Tee—a few times, and I'll come to you. I am able to do this, and I can help you in different ways so you won't be scared anymore or give up when things are hard. You have always been in my heart. I love you very much, and now I'm here as your guide to help you grow and know, just like my teacher did with me so very long ago."

"**N**ow I would like to tell you about our ancestors. They were some of the first beings to live here in this vast universe of ours. They had long, diagonal-shaped heads that were pointed at the top. Their bodies varied, and each person's body was a mixture of colors different from everybody else's."

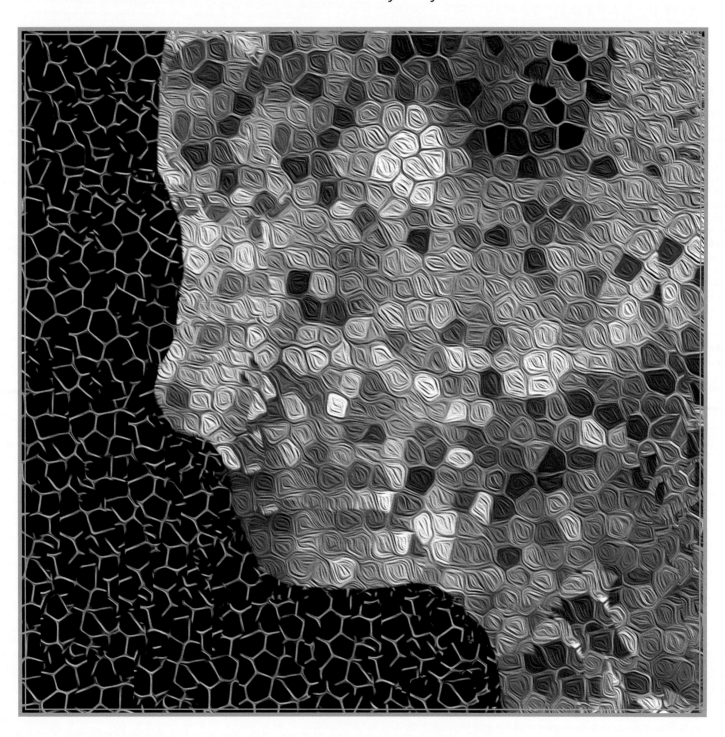

"They could levitate and remain in the air for short time. They had a very special ritual that they all followed. Each day, a different family member would take their turn at going outside and levitating while holding a torch up to the sky.

Hugh asked, "Why did they do that?"

Teebar said, "It was like a *prayer* for them. They did this to help them stay humble and respectful of one another and to be grateful for the gift of life."

"The torch represented the 'flame of love,' or desire in their heart to pass along knowledge and wisdom to others. And levitating was a symbol for raising their awareness or understanding to a higher level. These early people knew that being alive was a great blessing, a most precious thing. And because they practiced this ritual each day, they all experienced greater amounts of *love* coming into their life in many different ways, both simple and mysterious.

"One day, a being of almost pure white light appeared to them, wearing a hat with a feather pointing to the sky. He spent much time traveling around *The Worlds of Color*, showing all the people how to travel freely through space and time on the *eternal waves of love* so they could experience and know about other life forms existing throughout the universe. The ancestors tried this method, but only a few succeeded. Those few experienced a great sense of freedom and adventure plus a greater feeling of love and appreciation than they had ever imagined. Their awareness of life had grown, and because they felt such joy, they wanted to help the others have that experience too. Eventually, over a very long period of time, all the ancestors learned the art of traveling through space and time. This happened mostly because the ones who could do it had helped those who couldn't."

"So now, all the ancestors were experiencing more freedom, adventure, love, and appreciation than ever before. And because of this wonderful change that took place in them all, a very amazing thing happened … Their long, pointed heads began getting smaller, and they also lost their point at the top."

"This very slow process went on through many generations of ancestors. But when it finally did happen, all the people had come to the same understanding: they no longer needed the old ancestors' ritual of *levitating while holding a torch to the sky* to remind them to be humble and respectful of one another and grateful for the gift of life. Because now the people had evolved to the point where they could find love everywhere, both outside and inside of themselves. But out of a deep respect for their ancestors with long, pointed heads and to never forget the ancient ritual they had followed, this new generation of ancestors each wore a hat with a feather pointed upward, like the being of pure white light who taught the people how to travel through space and time. This nameless being had been *the one* responsible for helping so many generations of our ancestors grow, find more love, and share it with one another."

"It was during this ancient period of time in *The Worlds of Color* that you and I met and became close friends. We were part of this new generation of ancestors. We loved going down by the ocean to look for shells and watch the birds flying around. We often saw the same three birds together—the golden-orange, the red, and the black ones."

"It was always exciting for us to climb near the top of a mountain range and look down onto the birds flying below us."

"One of our most favorite places to visit was the *Pointed-tip Mountains*. That was the only spot in *The Worlds of Color* where people could visit to see the sun's double reflection over the water, no matter where the sun was in the sky. And none of the ancestors ever understood how that could be possible."

"At nighttime, we often stayed at the beach just to catch the moon disappearing behind a cloud and then reappearing as two different-colored moons of different sizes. We had fun trying to guess what colors the moons would be, but we hardly ever guessed right."

"Along the beaches and mountain paths that we traveled, we found feathers everywhere. There were so many different kinds of birds with varied colors."

"In your home, you had a flower that always seemed to attract butterflies when the flower turned bright-yellow and orange."

"You and I also met Noom, a tiny white being whose head looked like the moon and had a body made of tiny squares. We often saw him flying wildly all around the moon. You told me that once you looked at a large, bright star in the sky for a long time. Something about that star kept attracting you."

"Then Noom appeared from out of the star. He flew down to talk to you about some very *unusual* things, but you had no interest in knowing about them then.

"But I was very interested in the things he spoke about. He became my teacher and met with me many times. From him, I learned how to visit my past and see possible future events, how to disappear and reappear, and how to keep the same body. The way you see me now is the way I looked long ago when we were friends. Noom also showed me how I can be anywhere in the universe I desire. I'm able to be with you any time, but *only* if you invite me. These moments from our past that I share with you remain very warm, loving memories for me."

"I know you don't remember them, but sometimes it's helpful to go back and visit the past."

"Why?" asked Hugh.

Teebar said, "To simply learn some important lessons, such as why we have fears or bad habits today. A lot of our problems today are a result of how we acted or thought in the past. It is possible to see one's past, but what's more important is living in this very moment, *right now*, and being as aware as you possibly can. So always keep your eyes and ears open.

"Our ancestors, from that time we were friends, were peaceful people. They lived in a tropical climate. Their soil was rich with lots of colors, and their trees grew very large with a wide variety of colored leaves, wonderful-smelling flowers, and delicious fruits.

"The Tree with Many Colors that you fell asleep under was brought to earth and planted ages ago, long after the time we knew each other. It was the last remaining tree from our ancestors before *The Worlds of Color* ended from a number of natural disasters that occurred. The tree that they brought contained the *love* of all the ancestors and was planted as a gift to keep the *spirit of love* alive."

"And now it's time to end our meeting. When you return home, write down whatever you can remember about this dream. But don't worry if you forget things because there is a *higher* part of you that never forgets. Also, make three lists: (1) a list of things you are grateful for, (2) a list for ways you can give to others, and (3) a list of things that make you happy to be alive. Look over these lists from time to time. You will find them most helpful. And remember this: each answer you write down is a *gift of love* that has been given to you to help you grow and enjoy life more.

"Before we say goodbye, here's a *happy song* you can sing to remind you of being with me and to always look for ways to *give and receive love.* Sing it any way you like."

Tee and me
Me and Tee
Love is what he's teaching me

Love is here
Love is there
I *seem* to find it everywhere

Finding love is fun for me
And *easy* when I'm with Tee

Hugh awoke from his dream with Teebar. He got up from under The Tree with Many Colors and just stood there looking at the tree for a very long time with a deep feeling of gratitude and love. Then he hurried home to write down whatever he could remember from his dream. He had learned so many things being with Teebar, and because his dream was so real and meant so much to him, he remembered quite a bit.

Over the next few days, weeks, and months, Hugh studied his dream notes repeatedly. Sometimes, in other dreams at night, he would remember things from being with Tee. He wrote these down so he wouldn't forget. He often sang the *happy song* he was taught. Each day, he would practice at least one way of *giving*, like saying *kind* things to others. He also tried not to get angry with himself when difficult situations started to bother him. This was the hardest thing for him to do, but he kept trying and never gave up. He slowly began to appreciate more and more things in his life and noticed that he was becoming happier than ever before. As the years passed and he grew into an adult, Hugh still remembered and carried in his heart the many things Teebar had taught him. Then one day, he was very surprised to discover that he really understood and knew that he *is* love, that everyone and everything is love, and that only love exists.

Teebar, his ancient friend and teacher, still comes to visit him, especially when Hugh sings "Tee" or just thinks of him with love. They have never parted.

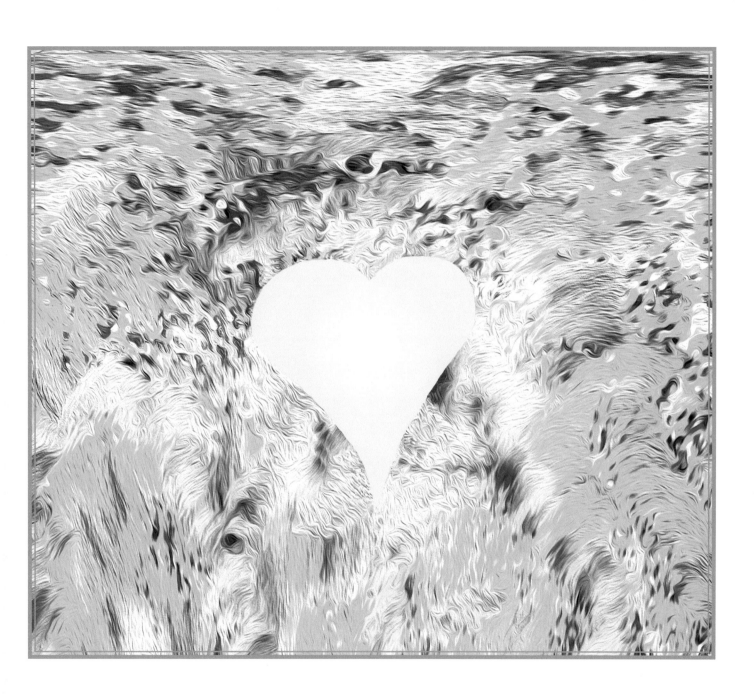

About the Author...

Fred Lipsius was the original saxophonist, arranger, and conductor with the popular jazz/rock group "Blood, Sweat & Tears" (1967-71). He won nine Gold Records with the band plus two Grammy Awards: one for 'Best Album of the Year' and another for his arrangement of the hit song "Spinning Wheel."

Fred produced, composed/arranged music, and performed on over 30 CDs, authored 7 books/CDs on jazz improvisation (published worldwide), toured with Simon and Garfunkle in Japan and Europe (1982), wrote music for TV and radio, and gave over 100 performances playing saxophone and piano at nursing homes, hospitals, and senior citizens homes around Boston.

Fred was born in the Bronx, New York City in 1943. He attended Music and Art High School in Manhattan, and then Berklee School of Music for a short time before going on the road, playing with different musical groups.

He's been creating digital art since 2004 and has had several showings of his work around Boston.

In January 2020, Fred retired from "Berklee College of Music" in Boston, after teaching for 35 years.

Fred has 2 websites:
fredlipsius.com
fredlipsiusart.com

He has numerous YouTube videos of his music, art, and interviews.

Contact: fredlipsiusbooks@gmail.com

Printed in the United States
By Bookmasters